Marquis of Lorne

Guido and Lita

A Tale of the Riviera

Marquis of Lorne

Guido and Lita
A Tale of the Riviera

ISBN/EAN: 9783337086442

Printed in Europe, USA, Canada, Australia, Japan

Cover: Foto ©Andreas Hilbeck / pixelio.de

More available books at **www.hansebooks.com**

GUIDO AND LITA

A TALE OF THE RIVIERA

ORLES.   [*Frontispiec*

GUIDO AND LITA

A Tale of the Riviera .

BY
THE RIGHT HON. THE MARQUIS OF LORNE

WITH ILLUSTRATIONS.

NEW YORK
MACMILLAN AND CO.
1875

" From countless terraces, where olives rise,
Unchilled by autumn's blast, or wintry skies."

[Page 2.

GUIDO AND LITA:

𝔄 𝔗𝔞𝔩𝔢 𝔬𝔣 𝔱𝔥𝔢 ℜ𝔦𝔟𝔦𝔢𝔯𝔞.

AIL, Riviera! hail, the mountain range
That guards from northern winds, and seasons'
change,
Yon southern spurs, descending fast to be
The sun-lit capes along the tideless sea;
Whose waters, azure as the sky above,
Reflect the glories of the scene they love!

Here every slope, and intervening dale,
Yields a sweet fragrance to the passing gale,
From the thick woods, where dark caroubas twine
Their massive verdure with the hardier pine,
And, 'mid the rocks, or hid in hollowed cave,
The fern and iris in profusion wave;

From countless terraces, where olives rise,
Unchilled by autumn's blast, or wintry skies,
And round the stems, within the dusky shade,
The red anemones their home have made ;
From gardens, where its breath forever blows
Through myrtle thickets, and their wreaths of rose.

Like the proud lords who oft, with clash of mail,
Would daunt the commerce that the trader's sail
Had sought to bring, enriching and to bless,
The lands they plagued with conflict and distress,
Till none but robber chiefs and galley slaves
Ruled the fair shores or rode the tranquil waves,—
So stand their forts upon the hills ; with towers
Still frowning, sullen at the genial showers,
That, brought on white-winged clouds, have come to dower
The arid soil with recreative power.

No warrior's tread is echoed by their halls,
No warder's challenge on the silence falls.
Around, the thrifty peasants ply their toil
And pluck in orange groves the scented spoil
From trees, that have for purple mountains made
A vestment bright of green, and gold inlaid.
The women, baskets poised above their brows,
In long array beneath the citron boughs
Drive on the loaded mules with sound of bells,

Turbia's trophy stamped the tyrant's will.

[Page 4.

That, in the distance, of their presence tells,
To springs that, hid from the pursuing day,
Love only Night; who, loving them, doth stay
In the deep waters, moss and reed o'ergrown,—
Or cold in caverns of the chilly stone,—
Sought of the steep-built towns, whose white walls gleam
High 'midst the woods, or close by ocean's stream.

Like flowering aloes, the fair belfries soar
O'er houses clustered on the sandy shore;
From ancient battlements the eye surveys
A hundred lofty peaks and curving bays,
From where, at morn and eve, the sun may paint
The cliffs of Corsica with colours faint;
To where the fleets of haughty Genoa plied
The trade that humbled the Venetian's pride,
And the blue wastes, where roamed the men who came
To leaguer tower and town with sword and flame.
For by that shore, the scene of soft repose
When happy Peace her benison bestows,
Have storms, more dire than Nature's, lashed the coasts,
When met the tides of fierce contending hosts;
From the far days when first Liguria's hordes
Stemmed for a while the rush of Roman swords,
Only to mark how, on their native hill,
Turbia's trophy stamped the tyrant's will;
To those bright hours that saw the Moslem reel
Back from the conflict with the Christian steel.

These last were times when, emulous for creed,
And for his soul to battle and to bleed,
The warrior had no need of pilgrim's vow,
At eastern shrines, to lay the Paynim low;
For through the west, the Saracen had spread
The night that followed where his standards led.

Not with the pomp or art Granada saw
Reign in her lands, beneath the Prophet's law,
Did the rude pirates here assert their sway :—
No gilded talons seized the quivering prey;
Savage the hand, and pitiless the blow,
That wrought the swift and oft-recurring woe.
No boon, no mercy, could the captive ask;
If spared to live, his doom the deadly task
To strain—a slave—each muscle at the oar
That brought the rover to the kinsman's door,
Or bore him, safe from the pursuit, away,
The plunder stored, to Algiers' hated bay.

With the dread terror that their raids instilled
Sank every hope, by which the heart is filled
Among the poor to labour and to hoard;
And e'en the merchant, for his gains adored,
Dared not to venture, or to gather more,
Where danger's form seemed darkening all before.(¹)
Only in narrow streets, where guarded wall,

And high-raised watch-tower gave the signal call
When foes were near, to gather in defence,
Did the scared people wake from impotence :—
And yet, neglecting what could give them power,
In jealous feuds they spent the prosperous hour;
While only adding to their grief's great load,
Each baron kept within his strong abode.
Careless of wars that yielded little prize,
They let the havoc spread beneath their eyes;
Content, if driven from their own estate,
The baffled spoiler sought another's gate.
Thus, through disunion, and their selfish greed,
The Moor, unharmed performed his venturous deed.
These Alps, the fastnesses of high Savoy,
Became his home; these fertile plains his joy.

E'en now the sounds of his barbaric speech
In many a word, his lingering influence teach;
For men will copy, 'neath a yoke abhorred
All, save the art to wield the conqueror's sword!

Whence then the strategy, or force, or guile,
That bade foul Fortune turn at length, and smile
Upon a region like a very heaven,
But vexed by man with hatred's cankering leaven?
See, where the mountain stretches forth a limb,
Down to the full sea's palpitating brim,

Dividing by that brawny arm the plain,
Just where a river swiftly seeks the main;
Upon the topmost ridge of its clenched hand
Appears a castle, strongest in the land.
From the hard rock the grisly ramparts rise,
Their front illumined by the morning skies:
And, sweeping from their broadening base away
The line of wall, the burghers' hope and stay,
Encircles with low towers the stony mass
Where, densely packed, the dwellings heap the pass;
And girdling still the fast-descending steep,
Crests the last ridge that overhangs the deep.

Beneath the cliff the fishing vessels float
With long-winged sails o'erarching every boat,
But where the river's mouth has made a port,
Guarded to seaward by yon square-built fort,
And near the rocks without the harbour bar,
Rise taller masts, with many a stronger spar.
On the broad decks that bear them may be heard
From time to time, the sharp commanding word;
But oftener far the sounds that meet the ear
Are the rough songs that tell the soldier's cheer,
The laughter loud and long, the shouted jest,
The tireless clamour of his time of rest,
When Danger draws not nigh, with finger cold
Enforcing silence on her followers bold.

Yet these are men who, if there come affront,
Seem ready now to bear her sternest brunt :
For some are polishing their arms, that shine
In fitful flashes o'er the sparkling brine ;
And some have landed, and in order move
Past the dark belts of yonder ilex grove ;
Or, stationed singly, drill and fence with care,
And hew with sword and axe the glancing air.

Now, on the road that leads from out the town,
Appear two knights, who slowly wend them down,
Till reached the ground, where still the men-at-arms
Repeat the mimicry of war's alarms.
But when among them wave the chief's gay plumes,
Each, in the ordered line, his place assumes ;
And waits, with steadied gaze, and lowered brand,
Till every weapon in each rank is scanned.

The elder knight, whose fierce and haughty mien
In his firm stride, and on his brow was seen,
Was grizzled, swarthy, and his forehead worn
By scars of fight and time, not lightly borne ;
For the dimmed eye that gazed, deep-sunk, beneath,
Showed that the spirit's blade had worn its sheath ;
And that full soon the years must have an end
In which, on friend or foe, that glance should bend.
The younger man, who followed at his side,

Bore the same impress of a lofty pride.
But all his bearing lacked the rigid mould
That in the elder of tough metal told;
Thus as the sire, with patient care, surveys
How every movement practised skill displays;
The son would saunter heedlessly along,
His lips just murmuring as they shaped a song.
His large grey eye was restless as the thought
That fixed no purpose in the mind it sought.
One jewelled hand was on his dagger laid,
With pointed beard the other often played,
Or swept from neck and shoulder curls that, flung
In studied negligence, upon them hung.
Yet though he seemed irresolute and weak,
A flush of pride would rise upon his cheek,
When his sire chid him, "as a stripling vain,—
Almost unworthy of this gallant train,"
And told him, if he cared not for such state,
To "go, play ball within the castle gate!"
Then backward falling for a little space,
· A pain was pictured on his handsome face:
The dark brows met, the shapely lips were pressed,
The nostril curved, as if for breath distressed.
But, as a glistening wave that quickly flies
From the cloud-shadow where its brightness dies,
To travel, laughing, onward as before,
With not a sign of any change it bore;

Did the light temper of the comely knight
Forget in joyousness the father's slight;
And smiling, answered, "Nay, my lord, you ne'er
Let me see use, in all this pageant fair;
For, save upon the field of their parade,
These gallant soldiers never bare a blade."
"Enough," the father answered, "that they keep
Our home from outward harm or treason deep,
And that you only hear, and have not seen,
Aught of what they in other days have been,
Before I made the town and yonder rock
Proof to the miseries you would lightly mock."

Thus speaking, with a few of their armed band
The two passed slowly to the yellow sand,
Listening the while to wants of those who came
To offer homage, or prefer a claim.
When free, as onward on their path they went,
The elder told how all his days were spent
"Throughout his youth, and e'en to manhood's prime,
In broils, the passion of his troubled time;
How, at the last, through many a year of toil,
Through the dread discord sown upon the soil,
He reaped the profit of his stubborn will,
And gathered power; until he won his fill
Of all for which a man of spirit strives;—
Riches and strength to save or take, men's lives.

'Twas true, all this might yet be still increased ;
But age had come, and his ambition ceased.
He would not care himself to waste more blood
By hunting those who ne'er against him stood.
They said the Saracen should be destroyed;
Then let them do it. If they died, he joyed.
Yet for himself he would not aid, for they
Had never dared to meet him in affray.
They knew the length of his good arm too well.
No, for his part, he felt no shame to tell,
His work had only been with those who dwell
Around and near him, thus his son had gained
Such place and power as none before attained.
He could not tell him how to use it, when
New times must change so much both things and men.
One maxim only he must bear in mind,
Aye to the followers of his house be kind,
For if the tree would stretch its branches round,
The roots must clasp and win the nearest ground."

The other, as such speech continuous flowed,
But little interest in his bearing showed.
His gentle nurture had not made him feel
Either the fear or love of brandished steel ;
And he but lazily would dream of deeds
Such as, with other youths, rapt fancy feeds,
Until the thought to glorious action leads.

Thus little had he cared for aught beside
The early objects of a boyish pride :
His sports, his horse, his dogs ; and now full-grown,
Less worthy loves seemed in his nature sown,
And less a man than when he was a boy,
A trivial foppery became his joy :
His velvet stuffs, the fashion of his sleeve,
His hat and plume, were what could please or grieve.
While thus he listened not, but gazed or sung,
His eye had wandered to where now there hung
Along the far horizon, a low cloud
That mounted steadily on high, while loud
The wind piped, like a rustic at his toil,
Furrowed the sea in ridges like the soil,
And scattered raindrops, as he strode along.
Then rose the storm, in awful fury strong.
Gleams of a wondrous light a moment stood
On pallid sea and on wind-stricken wood,
And dazzling, where they shone the vision's sense,
They fled ; and, chased by shadows as intense,
Passed with the swiftness of the blast, and leaped
From gulf to cliff,—then to the crags, that heaped
In grandeur 'gainst the flying skies, appeared
Like to white ashes that the fire has seared.
And then the mists rolled over them, as black
Grew heaven's vault with darkest thunder wrack ;
From under which, increasing in fierce sound,

A harsh and hissing noise spread fast around,
And a low moaning, like a voice of dread,
Welled, as if coming from the deep sea's bed.
The rain ran down, and, as the lightning flashed,
In bounding torrents o'er the ground was dashed.
From the dry hills the new-born fountains sprung,
The narrow tracks with swelling waters rung,
And, 'mid the turmoil could be faintly heard
The heavy fall of distant land-slip, stirred
To headlong ravage, burying as it flowed,
Man and his works beneath a hideous load!
Down the broad bed of shingle and of stone
That the shrunk river seemed ashamed to own
When, in the heat of the life-parching day,
A feeble streamlet, scarce it found a way ;
Now dashed a brimming tide, whose eddies surged
Till o'er the banks, the muddy foam was urged,
And louder still the notes of terror grew,
Ere past the hills the roaring tempest flew,
And on lashed sea, and groaning shore was spent
The rage of nature, and her frown unbent!

Meanwhile the old man would have held his way,
Unhurried, back to where the castle lay,
Now hidden long by headlands of the bay ;
But that they told him, "he must seek some rest ;
A fisher's hut was near, his shelter best."—

And to the joy of the gay plumaged knight
Who followed, sorrowing at their draggled plight,
They turned aside ; and, 'neath the slackening rain,
Soon found a cottage in a wooded plain ;
And passing through the open door, were met
By the poor owner, who, with garments wet,
Stood, dripping like a merman, standing nigh
The pine-wood fire, that sent its flame on high :
While the good wife, her distaff laid aside,
Still fed its glow with many a branch well-dried,
Chattering as o'er her task she bent intent,
And from the blaze a storm of sparks was sent.

A bright-hued sash the fisher's jerkin bound.
His scanty locks a crimson bonnet crowned.
He turned upon the guests a face that spoke
A ready welcome, ere he silence broke.
Then, with bared head and smile of joy, he said,
"Ah! knight of Orles, what chance has hither led
Thee and the Signor Guido ?—Enter here :
Praise be to God, and to the Virgin dear ;
May She from tempests every ill avert,
Send gladness as to me, instead of hurt !—
Pray, glorious sirs, to honour my abode,
And with deep gratitude my heart to load
By wishing well to me and this my roof :
Now of such kindliness to give me proof,

I pray you take your seats, and break your fast.
'Tis your first visit here, I fear the last,
For humble folk get not such favors oft :"
And here his dame broke in—"Hist! Carlo, soft,
Their presence now gives joy, and they may take
Some fish, and fruit, and wine. Our girl will bake
A little flour upon the embers soon :
Come hither, Lita—Lita. Here's a boon,
A pleasure rare for thee. Thy bread shall be
Refreshment to these lords of high degree.
O Signors, 'tis indeed a poor repast,
But on its winning has our toil been cast.
Come, Lita—wherefore lingers she?" Then came
Into the ruddy light of her hearth's flame,
So that it blazoned her young beauty forth,
And seemed to love with all its charms to play,
The fisher's daughter, pride of cape and bay!

Whose loveliness, not such as in the north
Blushes like sunshine through the morning mist,—
Was that of southern eve, quick darkening, kissed
By crimsoned lightnings of her burning day.
A maid whose arching brow, and glancing eyes,
Told of a passing, timorous surprise ;
Whose tresses half concealed a neck that raised
A head that classic art might well have praised.
Framed with the hair, in glossy masses thrown

From forehead whiter than Carrara's stone,
Her face's lineaments, clear cut, and straight,
Might show that sternness lived her nature's mate,
Did not the smile that over them would steal
Another mood, as favourite, reveal;
Else had not dimples on the sunburned cheek
Helped the eye's merriment so oft to speak.
O'er beauteous mouth and rounded chin there strayed
The sign of power that ardent will betrayed;
But broken by a gentleness of soul
That through her steadfast gaze in softness stole.
Her form was strong and lithe. She came and made
A slight obeisance, as though half afraid;
Then stood,—a coarse robe flowing to her feet,
Each limb round shadowed in the fitful heat.
And, like the glow that lighted her, there sped
Through Guido's frame a pulse that quickly fled,
But left his breathless gaze to feed upon
The figure that, to him, like angel's shone.
Till the repast prepared, his father quaffed
A horn of wine; and turning, as he laughed,
Said to the wife, "A beauteous maid in truth
You give to serve us. That young man, forsooth,
Has, as you see, no eyes for food, because
They worship elsewhere with a mute applause.
Nay! is she gone? I spoke with little grace,
Else had not scared her from her 'customed place."

2

Then said the wife, "Oh, sir, we do not heed
If her fair looks to admiration lead
With such great folks as you, who cannot care
For fisher maidens, with your ladies rare ;
But oftentimes, when neighbours come about,
They find my welcome marred by anxious doubt."
And Guido smiled, but could not laugh away
The spell of silence that upon him lay.

When, turning from old Carlo's poor abode,
The knights again together homeward strode,
So strange the feeling that within found birth,
It seemed to him he scarcely walked the earth.

One thought could only claim his wondering mind,
Alone once more that humble hearth to find,
Alone once more that radiant face to scan,
And prove the charm, as when it first began.

Ah ! who can tell, when thus the will is swayed,
And to emotion's dangerous train is laid,
The torch, that love or passion each can fire,
What hidden issue waits the heart's desire ?
What little grains the balance may control,
E'en though it shape the fortune of the soul,
That, by its fervid longings all possessed,
Yearns for the secrets of another's breast ;

Would live or die, but in the sight of one
Who to its being, seems the central sun,
Without whose presence every scene is drear—
The world a desert, haunted but with fear!
Who from the scroll of Fate may knowledge wring
Of the first birth of Life's mysterious spring,
What is the nature that so soon has grown
A potent tide, on which our bark is thrown?
Ah! who can tell if noblest impulse lies
Within the magic of the meeting eyes,
Or, if the ruin of a life be where
The light falls softest on some golden hair?

The knights of Orles regained the lofty keep,
When, sinking slowly on the purpled deep,
The sun still lingered on the bannered tower,
Though evening on the shore now showed her power,
And bathed it deeply in the twilight hour.

HOUGH the dark watches of the silent night
Must awe the soul that marks their solemn flight,
When myriad worlds, through boundless ether
   rolled
Their steadfast orbs, or trembling stars unfold;
And yon bright Mystery that in waning, proves
Her sway more potent, than the floods she moves,
Streaks with quick fire the rebel billows' foam,
When 'neath the rule of rival storms they roam;
Or looks serenely down, when calms display
Her image, multiplied in long array,
And o'er the waters, manacled in sleep,
Casts her white arm, as mistress of the deep;—
Yet are these hours the little space our mind
Regards as lulling into rest mankind:
They seem the pauses in our endless strife,
The only hours allowing peace, and life;
Oblivion comes to dull the subtlest brain
That schemes for honour, or has plotted pain,
Within these hours, that seem alone to beat
With no fierce pulses and no fevered heat.

And though this be not; and the night conceives
Things that the wondering morn accepts, believes:
Yet is her time less awful than the glow
Of eastern skies, that in their brightening show
The coming of the day, for weal, or woe.

Though still the air, and chill,—behold, behold
The hues of saffron deepening into gold;
Save where a sapphire band on ocean's bed
Along the far horizon lies outspread,
The heaving surface takes the tints on high,
And wakes its pallor to a kindred dye;
A moment more, and from the dusky hill
The vapours fall, the lower glens to fill;
Then fade from thence in many a changing shape,
To clasp the feet of every jutting cape;
Till the tall cliffs' descent into the sea
Is merged in mist, that makes them seem to be
Raised like the prows of galleys, that of yore
Stretched their proud beaks above the surges' roar.
Another instant, and each doubtful shade
Melts and then vanishes, as though afraid
Of the great blaze, unbearable, the sun
Sends o'er the world, proclaiming Day begun.

His reign is come, to last from morn till eve,
Within whose limits many live to weave

The fateful actions few can e'er retrieve :
His span of light, in which they can pursue
The petty plans that fill their narrow view ;
That yet have scope enough, through love or hate,
To make their working to their fellows great,
And in God's scales to place another weight !

Let the light shine on those, above whose graves
The deathless laurel of fond memory waves,
Who, though their age has passed away so long
Live in the glories of their country's song.
Let us then know the scenes, where varying fate
With partial hand, apportioned their estate.

But ere we reach the castle, note how well
The steep approach a foe's attack could quell.
'Twas not alone the battlemented wall,
With frequent tower, from whence the shot might fall ;
But every dwelling, in each close-built street,
Seemed half designed such venture to defeat.
High-storied, oft they over-arched the way
That, lost beneath them, scarce could see the day
For many a gloomy stretch ; and when at last
It seemed the devious labyrinth was passed,
'Twas only for a moment that the sky
Might look upon its course of mystery ;
(Save where before an ancient church there played,

In a broad space, a fountain's bright cascade ;)
For, quickly buried, it was hid until,
Beyond the town, it climbed again the hill.
Through the thick maze, a busy hive, close-pent,
Wound narrow tracks, that seemed where'er they went
With women, children, men, and mules, alive :
Some would pass quickly onward, but to dive
Beneath the vaulted arches; wives would spin
Chattering in doorways ; while, around, the din
Of little urchins rose, high shrilled, and clear,
Redoubled at the sight of muleteer,
But hushed as knights and guards came trampling near.

Close to the summit of the peopled ridge
The road led suddenly to where a bridge
Across a deep ravine, was lightly set.
Thin-arched and high, and void of parapet,
It spanned the chasm to the rough rock throne,
From which the castle's mighty limbs had grown.

No barbican o'erlooked the natural moat :
The way leaped straight into the fortress' throat.
The entrance through a square-built pile was bored,
Where, on each flank, a rounded bastion soared.
Their massive face of masonry but showed
A casement, here and there, toward the road.
But, circling inner courts, wide galleries ran,

Where through the open windows one might scan
The halls and stairways of the inner plan.
Throughout the spaces near the ponderous gate
Old halberdiers and armoured followers wait:
They guard the passages and line the hall
For stately trial or high festival;
When to give sentence, or to pass decree,
The knight was seated 'neath the canopy
Betokening feudal sway, that only saw
Justice in him who made, and dealt the law.

What is possession of high place, or state,
To him who, mocked by a pursuing fate,
E'en in his genius finds a dangerous bar
To turn his steps from Fortune's trembling star;
The finer temper that should make him rise
To be the leader in some great emprise;
To point the path, though mountains interpose,
To days of glory that no night may close;
May warp to tame fastidiousness, and wake
Loathing of tools, he might have used to make
His phantom fancy change to sober truth.
The easy nature, born of affluent youth,
To be content with all around, lest change
Shall bring upon him things unloved and strange,
May wake no passion for the prompt redress
Of wrongs he only hears have wrought distress;

" Till the tall cliffs' descent into the sea
Is merged in mist, that makes them seem to be
Raised like the prows of galleys, that of yore
Stretched their carved beaks above the surges' roar."

[Page 24.

Although if aid by clamorous grief be sought
Her piteous cry may wake to work and thought.

No chance had spurred young Guido to forget
The selfish aims to which his wishes set.
His father's rule, like some uncouth machine,
Creaked at its task, but worked in dull routine.
He hardly shared its burdens, for the chase
Gave him in sport at least a better place,
And often would his spear, haft-driven, quell
The rage of boar or wolf on mountain fell.
Yet lonely now, his part he would not bear
In scenes of pleasure, or in days of care.
Old friends, old joys, could give his life no zest,
Though to such charge his words had ne'er confessed.
In restlessness and yearning vain he spent
A time, when feigned hilarity was blent
With hours of brooding, on his thoughts intent.

How could he meet her, so that all unseen
His glance could rest upon her face and mien ;
That none should watch, or rally with a jest,
The sense that gladdened him, and yet oppressed?
He had not even heard her speak, then why
Dream that the voice would flow in harmony,
Nor give the ideal of his heart the lie,
Betraying aught to break its sympathy ?

What follies, treason, idle doubts, were these!
Whate'er the tone—how could she speak but please?
From the fair lips that curved like Cupid's bow,
Love's lightning darts through all she said must flow.
What, though the eyes no look responsive gave?
'Twas all he asked again their light to crave.

So, stealing furtively away, once more
He passed to where along the gleaming shore
The waves, like vassals of an eastern king,
In lengthened lines, continuous, came to fling
Their load of diamond and of opal down.

And as he quickly strode to clutch the crown
Of his heart's hope, it was as if for lord
The whole creation knew him, and adored.

So wild the tumult of his throbbing brain ;
It seemed the waters of that mastering main
But chanted songs that urged him to aspire
Until their motions owned but his desire ;
Whate'er his wishes' course, an answering God
Would smooth it level as the sands he trod.

Thus did his thoughts run riot till, afloat
Within three bowshots of the beach, a boat
With only one within it, could be seen.

Then inland moving, till he reached a screen
Of tumbled rock and wood, he saw below
A row of fishers, who, with labour slow,
Dragged heavily their nets' sea-laden length.
And, drawing nearer, he could see their strength
Was guided by the single boatman's call,
Who cried to them to slacken or to haul.
And further off, along the bay, appeared
Another group like theirs, that slowly neared,
As at the net's still great, but narrrowing, curve
They pulled with rival force and weary nerve.

'Twas Carlo's voice commanded them ; and soon,
In the full brightness of the blazing noon,
Guido saw Lita standing on the shore.

Upon her head and o'er her brow she wore
A kerchief, pure and white, to turn the glare,
From under which, escaping, the dark hair
In long rich tresses, flowed upon the vest
That clothed her form from ankle unto breast.

Poised on white foot that, light as foam-flake, fell
Where sea and land in common came to dwell,
She moved, encouraging with blithest cheer
Each laggard loitering at the toilsome gear.
Sometimes her little hand would even twine

A cord, loop-handled, round the great rope line,
And her slight aid, through their redoubled power,
Would shorten wondrously the arduous hour ;
Until at last, the scanty harvest reaped,
Its silvery piles upon the shore were heaped.

He had not thought to meet her thus among
Her kin and neighbours, and his sense was stung
By a commingling of delight and doubt.
He could not dwell upon her ways without
A shade of jealousy ; for though the voice
Rang in his ears, and bade his soul rejoice,
He had but pictured her in quiet home,
Not as one loving here and there to roam ;
Taking her part in harsher task, and made
A joy to many, but too oft displayed.

And yet what modesty of manner glowed
Through the quick nature that her gesture showed ;
What honest impulse 'mid the girlish grace
Lived in her word and shone within her face ;
E'en from her lips, when merriest laughter broke,
What innate dignity her bearing spoke !

She was not born to live her life away
In circuit bounded by her native bay ;
That beauty was not made to be the joy

Of common herdsman or of fisher-boy;
Surely from such companionship to win
Her sweet affection, were no mortal sin?
Let him then pass into the woods, and wait
Until she came to seal his wavering fate.

Alone he paused where, through the olive grove,
He saw the dwelling he had learned to love;
The door that opened to the lower space,
Where first he looked upon her witching face;
The outward stair that gained, still near the sod,
The upper chamber that her feet had trod;
The tinted plaster and the narrow roof,
Where heavy tiles to wind and rain were proof;
The gnarled and twisted trees that round it rose,
As if to guard its shelter and repose;
The dusky foliage where they thickly grew,
And chequered shade upon its brightness threw.

And soon along the pathway he could mark
Her form approaching 'neath the shadows dark:
And waiting by its margin, he could see
She slackened her quick step reluctantly:
Then made as though to pass him, and haste on
To where her home with friendly welcome shone.
When, doffing his plumed hat with courteous grace
And joyous look, he met her face to face.

Vain as he was, he felt at first unmanned
By the calm glance that all his motions scanned,
But when she slowly answered his good cheer
With morning greeting, he forgot his fear,
And questioned, "Whither went she?" "To prepare
For those who thro' the day have laboured where
You path does lead."—"Come they then soon to thee?"
"Yea, if they get enough from out the sea."
"Thou canst then give them all for which they care?"
"Nay, Sir, you know how humble is our fare."
"To me it seemed a feast for any prince."
"Our pride, indeed, has risen higher, since
Your gracious father said that he was pleased."
"And wilt thou not believe that I was seized
With gratitude to her, who, like the sun
Shone, when the storm dominion would have won?"
"Oh, Sir, you flatter me," she said, and then,
"But I must onward, or my father's men
Will find nought ready. Sir, I must begone."—
"Nay, have my words so little favour won,
Thou wilt not offer me again some food?"—
"If you desire it. 'Twould indeed be rude,
And 'gainst my father's wish to close our door."—
"It is but for a moment, and the store
Of thy sweet grace, is all I now implore."—
She laughed, and then, with grave and silent mien,
Led on, he following, o'er the herbage green.

And thus he entered, with a heart that beat,
The house wherein again her busy feet
Moved, as it seemed to him, in music sweet.
And as he sat, and watched how order grew
Beneath her fingers, as they deftly drew
Her tasks to end; her every look and word
His passion deepened, and his wonder stirred.
How could such blossom grow on salted soil,
Such bloom and beauty from a race of toil,
Such grace and colour near the deadening spray?
In childish days he heard the sailors say
That wondrous flowers were fostered by the ray
That burned on Afric's coast, and glowing leaves
Burst from the prickly plants in dazzling sheaves,
Close to pale breakers of a fearful sea.

Such vision rose within his mind as he
Noted her actions;—told her how his thought
Had, since he saw her, his lone spirit brought
To be a sojourner, as now, beneath
Her roof; marked how a fleeting blush would breathe
An instant's brighter colour on her cheek;
But pride or coyness would not let her speak
Reproof or pleasure. Then he drank to her
Of wine she offered, that he might aver
Her happiness was now his life's desire.
His hope to please her lived,—a beacon fire.

Then finding answer none, he sought to know
How simple ways could such distinction show.
He hearkened, half amused, as she would paint
In artless phrases how some favourite saint
"Upon the day named after him, had blessed
With draught of fish, miraculous (confessed
As such by e'en the very Priest himself),
The household nets ;—and thus, though for such pelf,
All knew the Father cared not, he had ta'en
Some coin and half the fish, lest luck were vain,
To buy a picture of the circumstance,
Wrought by a youth whose fame he would advance ;—
The Virgin-Mother watching from a cloud
The happy fishermen and clamorous crowd ;—
To hang upon the chapel's wall. And more :
At the last feast the candles borne before
The holy Father came from this, their wealth ;
Besides, what more went to the Church's health."

"But 'tis not from your nets," he said, "alone ⁕
You get your living, for you surely own
These trees that far around the sunlight break ?"
"No, no," she answered, "'tis but ours to shake
Their laden branches with the tapering cane
And cause the olives' fall of fruitful rain ;
To gather them in baskets till they fill
The dusty flooring of the busy mill.

But in a little garden, all mine own,
Some beauteous palms, beloved of God, have grown,
And of their drooping fringes I may keep
Some here, to grace the day of those who sleep
In martyrs' graves beyond the echoing deep :
Some for their place of martyrdom, I sell
To those, they say, who near their ashes dwell."
He, asking where this Eden garden lay ?
Watched her fair figure outlined 'gainst the day
That, through the open window near him, shone ;
And let her eager speech, unchecked, flow on,
As with her lifted hand, she pointed where
A palm-tree shot aloft to woo the glare :
Then showed each spot in narrow circuit round,
Where traces of her simple life were found.

But breaking through the tale of her content,
His stifled longing to her ear now sent
Its tones of praise, with fond entreaty blent :
And reaching out his arm that he might hold
Her hand, or only of her dress a fold
She shrank away from him,—if not with fear,
Yet with a start, as timid as the deer
Who first has seen the long-accustomed food
Offered by strangers, and in doubtful mood
Retires, distrustful for a space, to gaze
If it spy danger in their novel ways.

3

So in surprise, but feeling no dismay,
She stood and listened, for on many a day,
Her ears had heard the youths around her say
All that they thought would flatter or would please,
Till she ne'er wondered at such praise from these.
But he had startled her, and would have chased
Away the harsh remembrance of his haste
By soothing words; but as she silent stood,
They heard the fishers coming through the wood,
With noise confused within its solitude:
And whispering he would see her soon, he sped
Through tracks again that to the castle led.

Thus first did Guido drink of what he sought.
Yet was he like a thirsty wanderer, brought
To some rich fountain, rising in delight,
A rainbowed pillar to the raptured sight,
That falls again in such a gentle spray
Within a basin broadening to the day,
That scarce a ripple comes to sweep away
The face reflected on its surface, where
Unto the eager lips, the hands would bear
The copious treasure, of the guest aware.

He looked upon her beauty, and admired:
He drank therein of joy as he desired;
But while he stooped, his wishes to fulfil,
Himself he saw, and Self was master still.

His pride untutored, and by time unbent,
Saw in her silence only her consent;
Read in her blushes' consciousness alone
The sign of feelings, he might make his own;
Believed, (and half of what he thought was truth,)
That victory waited on his brilliant youth;
And with no shame there passed before his view
That poorest triumph man can e'er pursue:
The careless conquest of affections true
That woman gives, not knowing she may rue!

Already, almost to herself unknown,
An interest in her breast for him had grown;
And with surprise she sometimes found her thought
Muse on the morning that his presence brought,
And sought to check the question that would rise
How next to meet the searching of his eyes;
Denying he would come, and if he came,
By silence she would prove her will the same.

And for a while it thus to him appeared,
As often now that olive grove he neared
To intercept her on her homeward way,
And no persuasion could her footstep stay.
Yet had his manners, that with ease combined,
A pride by grace and gentleness refined,
Shown her the roughness of her fisher-folk,

Contrasted with the world to which she woke;
And his society had in time supplied
A lofty standard by which all were tried.

What wonder then, that she could not deny
That pleasure came with knowledge he was nigh?
No words of hers were uttered to persuade
That lingering partings should be yet delayed;
Perhaps because she saw such conduct made
The moments lengthen as he, dallying, stayed!

Still he, in blindness, could not comprehend
Whence came the firmness that to her could lend
Such strength of character, until the flame
That still consumed him, though it seemed the same,
Changed, with the light by admiration given,
To wear the radiance honour takes from heaven!
And with the homage that his bearing spoke,
In time her shy reserve was loosed, and broke.
Frank had she ever been, in all beside
The feelings sacred to a maiden's pride.
Open and true, e'en these were not concealed,
When safety whispered, they might stand revealed.

But the calm will, though shaken on its throne,
Still held the empire of her mind alone,   R
And gave sad answers to the doubts that pressed,

And with untimely grief her life distressed.
How could it profit him that she should love
One placed by fortune such regard above?
Would it not hurt him, rather, thus to bend
And to her level, from his own, descend?
Would his affection, now so fervent, last;
Contempt not come when novelty had passed;
If from his eyes the scales at length were cast?

Thus tortured by misgivings that but grew
Stronger, the nearer to his love she drew.
Faithful to that she deemed would serve him most,
She sought no more the pathway to the coast;
But would have hid herself, lest she might fill
And mar his life with some imagined ill.
'Twas therefore long before he could succeed
Again his cause with earnest tones to plead:
When to his sorrow, coldness seemed to reign
Within the breast where tender love had lain.
And crushed beneath the unexpected pain,
Tears, and upbraiding, and reproach, had sprung,
From the full heart, with pain and passion wrung.

Then roughly tried, there fled, dispelled at length,
The false illusion of her borrowed strength.
To see him thus was more than she could bear.
"Think not," she cried, "my words betray no care;

But what wild folly were it, did I dare
Thy lordly home, thy mighty name, to share?
The scorn of kindred, and the strangers' smile,
Would mark the action thou must soon revile.
God placed me here because He knows I may
Lighten with joy my parents' waning day.
How could I be an honour to thy race,
A lowly weed transplanted from its place?
Nay, hear me, Knight, for though my words are weak
'Tis only for thy good I dare to speak ;
And when a year has run its destined round,
A change, perchance, will in thy thoughts be found.
Oh, leave me—go!—nor let the memory live
Of one unworthy of the love you give."

"You trust me not," he answered, "Lita, mine,—
For mine I call thee,—since no force divine
I know, would ever part us ; and if Hell
Rise in dark legions, my pure love to quell,
What banded might shall overthrow the pride
This year shall give me, when I call thee bride.
Be my request but this : 'Tis not to hide,
Nor move from hence, if thus my troth be tried."
"'Tis best," she faltered, "that thou come not here."—
"No power shall keep me from a place so dear,"
He said ; and ere a week was passed, his eye
Looked on the scene, in wonder, to descry

Groups of the peasants scattered 'neath the trees ;
And crowds that stood around the door, and these
Seemed scared ; for, wafted on the breezy air
Rose the shrill plaint, and murmur of despair.

Some carried household goods, and women's tears
Flowed on, unheeding e'en the children's fears.
Others, from where a vessel, anchored, lay,
Landed in haste, and hurrying made their way,
Some to the woods, and some along the shore,
As though in peril safety to implore.

Then, stopping one who seemed in sore distress,
Guido demanded, "Wherefore do ye press
Onward, as though a foe were on your track ? "
The man, in silent horror, pointed back
To distant headlands, where arose a black
And spreading vapour he could well discern :
Then cried, "O see'st thou not our houses burn ?
The murdering fiends—O may their names be cursed !
Upon our sleeping towns at night have burst,
And all are massacred who could not fly ! "
"Take courage," said the knight, "our force is nigh."
"Yea," said the fugitive, "we know our lives
Here, at the least, are safe from murderous knives ;
But we, pursued by sorrow and by fear
Have lost the joys that made them once so dear.

Would that a wider space than this domain,
Were guarded by the men none dare disdain!
'Tis long indeed, we know, since Orles has seen
The fires of pillage light her nights serene."

Returning with the people, who now sought
Friendship, and shelter, in their state distraught,
He heard from many of their hard escape,
Whom Death had menaced in his direst shape.

'Twas from the mountains that the heathen horde
Upon the smiling Riviera poured,
Within a district, where deceitful Peace
Had blunted arms, as though their use might cease.
But for the darkness all had been undone :
Their ship had saved them ere the place was won,
And the bright flames, ascending, had begun
To guide the hunters, like a midnight sun.
Soon round the walls, and hospitably fed,
The victims told full oft their tale of dread ;
Or, harboured by the townsmen, scarce believed
Their safety certain, or their lives reprieved.
And ever ministering to those in need,
Lita wrought daily many a holy deed.

But loud and fierce among the exiles rose
The cry for vengeance, on their cruel foes,

As ever greater grew the ravage made
In distant homesteads, where the robbers' raid
Drew gold or blood, at will, from men dismayed,
And e'en to fight in their defence afraid :
Surely the knight of Orles will raise his hand
And be the saviour of a grateful land?

Yet soon they found their hope had woke in vain :
"These people were not his; not his their pain ;
They must not cumber his industrious folk.
They might remain a little. Then the yoke
Of Saracen or Pirate by the stroke
Of their own hands must perish. Why should he
Arm for the men who knew but how to flee ;
Who for themselves should learn that woes but yield,
When swords, not tongues are loosed, to win the field."

And Guido did not urge their suit, his own
Was in his thoughts ; and these were fed alone
By envious musings, how he might prevail
That Lita should not hearken to the wail
Of these poor wretches, through the livelong day.
He hated them that they should turn away
Her mind from him. And thus a month was passed
In idling leisure, till the Moors at last
Were said to be no longer in the land
And few remained of all the ruined band
Who sought in Orles for safety or for aid.

But amongst these, a youth the crowd outstayed,
Who oft had cheered them as he bravely played
To rhyming song the strings of his guitar.
He told of love, of chivalry in war,
Of feats that made world-famous oft of yore
The name Provence through lustrous ages bore;
And noting with contempt and fierce disdain
The knights' indifference to their want and pain,
Now 'neath the casemate of their proud abode,
He poured the verse that told his sorrow's load;
And boldly thus, though helpless, robbed, and poor,
Rung thy reproach, thou gallant troubadour !

I.

Noble names, if nobly borne,
    Live within a nation's heart:
If of such thou bearer be,
Never let that name for thee
    Point the scorn !

II.

Shrined within its narrow bound
    Other hopes than thine have part;
For it once in life was theirs,
Who from weight of earthly cares
    Peace have found !

III.

They who wore it, free from blame,
Set on Honour's splendid height,
Watch, as spirits, if its place
Love the night, or daylight's face,—
Shame, or Fame.

IV.

'Tis a precious heritage:
Next to love of God, a might
That should plant thy foot, where stood
Of thy race the great and good,
All thine age!

V.

Yet remember! 'tis a crown
That can hardly be thine own,
Till thou win it by some deed
That with glory fresh shall feed
Their renown!

VI.

Pride of lineage, pomp of power,
Heap dishonour on the drone.
He shall lose his strength, who never
Uses it for fair endeavour:
Brief his hour!

F those great attributes we call divine,
 The changeless Strength,—the Space, none dare
  define,
 How few the types, O mortal globe, are thine!

Thou hast but two pre-eminent, that bear
To our dim vision of these things a share,
The mountain and the sea ;—and of these twain
With one alone, does changelessness remain.

The heights seem made for ever, and abide,
Though glowing lava streak their trembling side,
And bursting craters shake to founts of fire,
Where, shaped in rugged dome, or massy spire,
They raise their forms into the azure air ;
What thing of grandeur may with them compare ?
Man may not measure by his thought of time,
The boundless ages since their birth sublime :
All else decays, whate'er his tongue can name,
But they remain, their majesty the same.
The fabling Greek would tell that wingéd hours

Kept guard for ever where Olympus towers
Above the rock-built chains, and ocean's foam,
And deemed his gods had claimed it for their home.
The Hebrew multitudes saw clouds enshroud
The God of Truth, with darkness, as He bowed
Himself o'er Sinai, and the hill became
His hall of audience, filled with sound and flame.
Sacred they seem, most sacred when their might
Is robed in raiment of untainted white;
When the keen airs that from their summits blow
Descend from freshened fields of virgin snow.

Then to the wearied wanderer's frame they give
A sense exultant of the joy to live;
A strength undreamed of, yea, not e'en by those
Whose boasted magic would relieve our woes,
And, by the essence of life-giving power,
Hold us, for ever, to Youth's fleeting hour.
With them lives Beauty undefiled and pure,
As in the life that shall for aye endure;
As radiant seems their promise, as unknown
The tracts between us, and each dazzling throne.
There must the pilgrim in his passage meet
Gaunt Peril waiting to arrest his feet.
Above the vapours o'er the valleys furled,
His mounting step reveals another world.
No lofty cypresses like sentries stand

O'er fruitful woods, the proof of generous land;
The barren pines, in sombre masses, climb
The slopes that echo to the torrent's chime.
From soaring peaks that to the stars convey
The secrets gathered from their wide survey,—
That seem the haunts of silent calm, until
The thunder commune with the answering hill,—
His gaze, descending to blue rifts, beholds
The glacier crawling in its glistening folds.

An icy menace! as though cruel eyes
Shone, keen and watchful, where it crouching lies:
Beneath the frozen cliffs' advancing feet,
From caverns where the prisoned waters meet,
The bursting floods in gladness to be free,
Sing from their hollows, as they downward flee;
Yet bear from cold captivity the stain
Those glittering vaults but seek to hide in vain.

On every side, at hand, or far away,
The naked barriers of the Alps display
Their varied outlines, while, half-veiled in haze,
A silver streak the distant sea betrays.

A fir-clad mound amid the savage wild,
Bears on its brow a village, walled, and isled
In lone seclusion round its ancient tower.

Here had the elements begun to lour,
That on the hapless coast would quickly shower
The horrors of a war of faith and hate.
It was a post of Saracens, whose fate
Made them the masters for long years of lands
Remote, and scattered o'er a hundred strands.

Within a journey compassed in a day
From Orles, a portion of their forces lay.
Towns had they by the sea, with ships and wealth ;
Some won by force, and some by treacherous stealth.
Rude captains on their frontier held their own,
Their lawless deeds scarce to each other known ;
But those of Sirad had been noted well,
As oft performed with all the art of Hell,
To spread the rule of Islam far and wide.
A grisly bigot he, who had denied
Himself no vices that his creed allowed,
At morn and eve his knee to Mecca bowed,
With prayer to Allah, that his servant's sword
Might purge the land for Mahomet and the Lord.
In Spain, he saw his haughty race deride
The pompous chivalry of Christian pride,
And burned to see the Crescent soar above
The darkened Image on the Cross of love.
Where'er he moved he kindled battle's fires,
And in its flames, he fashioned his desires.

'Twas he, on plunder and on slaughter bent,
Who led the raid, that into Orles had sent
The clamorous fugitives, whose piteous throng,
Demanded vengeance, fearful as their wrong.
Wild Rumour's whisper scarcely had averred
The aged lord had pledged to them his word,
To give them clothing in such nakedness,
And by reprisal cover their distress,
Before the infidel had vowed to dare
And beard their champion, in his chosen lair.

Through every settlement his couriers sped,
And quickly to his eyry backward led
A motley host of men, to war inured,
Who deemed that death but Paradise assured ;
The ocean pirates joined their strength, and planned
Enfolding horror for the sleeping land.

Before the entrance of his narrow gate,
Behold El Sirad for his followers wait.
Down from his shoulders falls a robe of green ;
In yellow swathed, his limbs below are seen.
A tunic, barred across the chest, is bound
By a broad belt, in glistening circle wound
O'er a long dirk and shorter poniard blade,
And slung a sword, sharp-curved, with hilt inlaid.
From 'neath his turban of the Prophet's hue,

His black eye brightens, as within its view,
Rise distant forms, the foremost of the crew,
The hastening bands, that herald as they speed
A swarm of villains, urged by bloodshed's greed.

Their column's van now fills the valley deep,
Now, struggling, breasts the last and nearest steep;
And as the rest in quick succession come,
Awaking with their shouts the desert dumb,
In broadening front, around, and at his side,
Their greeting sounds as wolves' to wolf allied;
They fill the space before him; armour shines
Between dark pillars of the mourning pines;
And hills, all silent in their shroud of snow,
Seem as though sorrowing o'er the scene below.

How varied this, in changing hues and shapes
The gaudy raiment that each warrior drapes,
The flashing of the scimitars and spears,
The swarthy features and barbaric cheers,
Bring to this spot, that Summer loves the least,
The warmth, the sparkle, of the glowing East.
Thronged on the ground before him, at his hand's
Uplifted signal, every soldier stands;
The swaying crowds are hushed from front to rear,
And forward bend, their chieftain's words to hear.

4

"Brethren, true comrades, who this day have shown
The prompt obedience Allah loves to own,
By list'ning to his servant's warning word;
Hark to my tidings, from sure sources heard:
The knight of Orles, too long in safety left,
Of his known prudence suddenly bereft,
Dares, as though arbiter of our disputes,
To turn our victories, and to spoil their fruits.
His power was left him, and he has the will
Our cup with dregs of bitterness to fill,
And mar the march of conquests that have sped
Untamed by numbers, and unknown of dread.
'Tis a just punishment, by Heaven given,
For in past years ye should with him have striven,
Then had his power ne'er gathered, till in peace
It swelled to menace with its dull increase.

His new presumption ye must now chastise,
But do not yet his fore-doomed might despise.
Though of my summons he is unaware,
And we, by rash attack, might downward bear
The first resistance, we might thus but heap
The well-trained masses o'er our heads, and keep
Their host united, and prepared to fall
With tenfold weight, should fair occasion call.
Sudden our blow should be,— but 'tis our pride
That counselling Wisdom walks at Valour's side:

Our unity shall now his strength divide.
To aid in this, we look to you, ye brave,
Whose steed of battle is the white-maned wave:
Ye from these odds shall Allah's standard save.
Yours be the part, in opening our campaign,
To lure our foe upon the treacherous main.
This is my scheme :—together we invade
In rapid onslaught—nought must be delayed—
The lands around the castle ; but your oars
Must flash in hundreds off the neighbouring shores :
All prisoners captured, and all goods we seize,
We here may lead, and guard them at our ease ;
But, to appearance, they must be conveyed
Across the seas by you : let sail be made ;
A captive freed, to whom this tale displayed,
That, carried to far colonies as slaves,
The winds shall mock their madness as it raves.
Then Orles shall man his fleet, and sailing, leave
But slender garrison ; while you will cleave
With your sharp prows the waters till the eve ;
Then turning under shelter of the night,
Wheel back, and join us for decisive fight,
While they at sea, shall make pursuit a flight."

He paused : a deep, excited murmur ran,
With looks of savage glee, from man to man ;
And then resuming : "Do you join," he asked,
"In these my projects? Is your zeal o'ertasked?"

"Nay! nay!" a thousand throats, as one, replied.
"Then swear with me," El Sirad loudly cried:
"Swear by the Prophet's head, by Koran's writ,
By this our bond, with holy fervour knit;
Swear as though prostrate in your mosques, and let
These mountains serve as dome and minaret,
To rest not, pause not, till the land be freed
From Christian dogs, from their accurséd breed."

"We swear!" The words like thunder, rose, and rung,
Each cliff attesting, with mysterious tongue
That oath, in wrath, to listening heaven flung.

As flowers are gay beneath a threatening sky,
So seemed it joy could never tire or die
Around the home, where, e'en if grief had paid
A fleeting visit, it had ne'er delayed;
But must have fled at one light word alone
From her whose doubting heart to none was shown.

Like fairy vessel, born of childhood's dream,
Lita, to those she loved, would often seem,
A bark, descended from the heaven above
With shining load of hope divine and love,
That shed such gladness, that the night would ope,
As though unable with its light to cope:
And only when it passed, had power to make
A distant darkness close behind its wake.

Still, though a sorrow sought her gentle breast,
No pining mood her father s hearth distressed.
Unselfish ever, as in other days,
She made mirth minister in artless ways
To lighten burdens, sprung from toil and age.
Oft, when the time of Advent would engage
The countryside, in fasting and in prayer,
To deck the altars with some flowerets fair
Was for the maidens all, a cherished care ;
And she would lead them to some pleasant glade
Where heath and cistus glowed in tangled shade ;
And all day long, with laughter, and with song,
They wove frail blossoms into garlands strong.

A pleasure 'twas, a joy no man might ask,
To watch them busied at their lovely task.
Their youthful forms would bend with pliant ease
To search among the time-unyielding trees,
Where clustering leaves the conquered soil had won,
For violets, sheltered from the scorching sun.

If flower could prey on flower, 'twould here be said
One host a kindred army captive led ;
But 'tis not flattery, nor true praise, that tries
To give a name that humbler worth implies
To what is best, and highest in our eyes.
What plant, though fair and wondrous to our view,

As if it drank the very rainbow's hue,
And gave the odours of celestial dew;
Can show the tender glories, such as brood
O'er those whom God leads on to womanhood?
What senseless life can vie with charms that spring
From minds, whom purity and gladness wing
To soar too high, for sorrow's shade to cling;
Or imitate the motions that afford
Fresh beauteous pictures which, in memory stored,
Live, though they vanish from our vision's field,
Replaced by others for a while revealed?

Some of this young and bright invading band
Had step as stately, as when first from land
A lofty ship glides slowly from the port,
The faint wind dallying with her sails in sport.
And others seemed so wrapped in happy haste,
'Twould pain their feet an instant's rest to taste;
But flitting ever on, from place to place
They strove, as if for life, to win the race,
Who could the fastest the sweet blossoms pull,
Whose kerchief heaviest, with its burden full.

Some pretty traitors would their harvest waste
In mimic warfare, as they swiftly chased,
Or fled in turn, before their friend's assault;
Or, when a moment, for a foe at fault,

They turned on those who gathering, busied, knelt,
With blows of soft and sudden treason, dealt
In odorous showers, that spangled all the glade,
Despite of peace proclaimed, and treaties made.
A score of shapely arms at work were seen,
Testing with rapid touch, each tiny screen,
If aught lay hidden 'neath its covering green:
And faces, flushed with merriment, would turn
The nearest rival's last success to learn ;
When, as the load was all complete, the sound
Of laughing triumph, told the feat ; and found
The maiden rise, with panting breast, to bound
To where some, seated in a circle, twined
The scented chaplets, for their saint enshrined.

And while the wreaths to greater volume grew,
And the quick hands the thread around them drew,
The voices of the weavers rose and fell,
As each some rhyme would sing, or story tell.
The birds themselves would from their lilt refrain
To list to tones of more harmonious strain,
And to the happy groups draw nearer still,
From woodland thicket, and from sunlit hill :

   The violet peeped above the snows
   First in Provence, when Christ arose ;
   Each year it comes that we may see
   A type of His nativity.

From near the season of His birth
Until His death it gems the earth ;
And to the lowly blossom clings,
The purple, that is worn by Kings!

Thus sang the leader lastly, as the end
Of their light labour came, and she would wend
Homeward, environed by her whole array.
But one still lingered, who loved far away
Alone to muse, or, plucking flowers, to stray ;
Why shrieking runs she to rejoin the rest,
As if a vengeful fate too hotly pressed?
All wait, as breathless, and with starting eyes
The flying girl comes near with fearful cries,
"What is it then : what means this strange surprise ?"
She gasps, "O fly! escape!" and terrifies
Her wondering comrades, who but stand and stare ;
Then, gaining speech, "The Saracens are there!"

They start, and turn, but instantly aware
Of many men's approach, they turn to find
Yet more advancing quickly from behind.
Then clasped together, trembling in despair,
Silent, so petrified they could not dare
Even to cry, much less than to exert
An effort vain their misery to avert ;
They waited dumb, as though to terror tame ;

When all around, from every side, there came,
As from the ground, the foes whose awful name
Formed the first dread their lisping childhood knew.

And as their phantomed horror rose in view,
Some sank to earth, and some, despairing, eyed
The coming bandits through the forest glide ;
As nearer yet they came, and yet more near,
Noiseless at first, and then with shout and jeer.
And as the girls shrank back in deadly fear,
Rough hands took hold and seized them fast, and bound
Their yielding limbs ; and o'er their ankles wound
Long cords, that tied them, so that two abreast
Might walk together.   Then with many a jest,
They closed around, and bade them march along.
The weak were dragged, and led the brave and strong
Down to the coast ; save three who, with a man
Captured at morn, were hurried to the van,
And freed, and watched, as on their way they sped,
To spread in Orles the story false and dread,
Feigned by the captors ;—that the prisoners ta'en
Might o'er the seas be sought, though search were vain.

Along the shore the fierce confederates ploughed
The angry shallows, with their galleys' crowd,
They passed, repassed, with ostentation loud,
As though their boats were bringing all away.

And waiting till the secret close of day,
Till the dim shades of early evening crept
From the grey sea, and e'en the mountains slept,
And all was hushed in silence for a time,
As if fair Nature helped her children's crime ;
The ships departed.   Then the bands on shore
Turned, and with haste the wretched women bore
A long march inland, through a forest hoar,
Heedless of tears, from eyes with weeping sore.

Then halting in the wood beside a brook,
The thongs and fetters from their limbs they took.
There Sirad marked again with fierce delight
The beauty Lita could not hide from sight,
And placed her on his mule, and at the head
Of the armed train himself his captive led ;
While she sat motionless without a groan,
As though her form were changed to senseless stone.
Her face was bloodless, and her eyes now wore
A strange, fixed look, that none had seen before ;
She answered not a word, as he would seek
To hear the accents of her terror speak ;
A tribute slight indeed to prove his power,
And yet desired, as though neglect to cower,
Concealment of her trembling at his ways,
Could injure him.   And then with sickening gaze
He tried her vanished hopes again to raise

By telling her what treatment good he gave
To virtuous damsels, for he well could brave
Danger, unmasked, their pleasant lives to save.

But Lita could not even loathing feel,
So bruised and pierced was she by misery's steel,
That sense seemed lost of what was woe or weal;
She felt indeed her consciousness benumbed,
As if sensation at the shock succumbed;
Yet knew a latent force still lived to fence,
And God would aid at least her innocence.

She could not count the time, but it was day
Before she heard the miscreants round her say,
A mountain village that before them lay
Was the last goal, to which their steps were bent.
Once more, by Sirad's order forward sent,
An arch was passed, and next she was aware
That the mule halted at a broken stair.
Told to alight, she found she was alone
Among her foes. Where were her comrades?—thrown
Already in some dungeon,—who could tell?
The loss, when learned, in part could break the spell
That held her passionless; she cried aloud:
"Where will ye take me?" But they only vowed
No harm should touch her; and, to all her prayers
That she might suffer with her friends;—"Who dares

To question Sirad's will?" they laughing said;
And brought her up the stairway that soon passed
Within a passage of thick walls, and last
Into a chamber where were carpets spread.

And left alone, she sank almost as dead
Upon the floor, and sobbed till slumber deep
Closed the dull eyes that ached but could not weep,
And hid from thought the future and the past
Behind the veil by sweet oblivion cast.
Exhaustion proved itself a potent friend,
And for a space her woes were at an end.

Who knows what gift that Nature gives at birth,
Weakness or strength the greatest boon on earth?
Our youth may triumph in abounding might,
Its loss be hateful in our longing sight;
But when misfortune comes, and in her train,
Brings mental anguish or exhausting pain,
The vigorous frame, whose spirit cannot yield,
Prolongs the torture of the doubtful field;
While feeble powers, that long from striving ceased,
Ensure the peace, they seemed to promise least.
Thus could this tender maid a while forget
The place that held her, dangers that beset;
And there could reach her, through a fence of stone,
An influence that should share her prison lone,

Passing the wary guard, unseen, unknown,
And stilling with sweet rest her piteous moan.

She slept, or was it but a dreadful swoon,
That made her lie so still at first?—but soon
If it were such, it passed into a sleep
With breathings low, and regular, and deep ;
And o'er the features drawn by anxious pain
A blessed contentment now began to reign.
The parted lips, and placid face, expressed
No sign that Trouble stayed within the breast,
The outer clamour of the hurrying feet,
That sounded loudly e'en in this retreat,
Ne'er entered the carved chamber of her ear,
Whose tender curve lay, delicate and clear,
Against the masses of the fallen hair ;
Like some rare shell that on the ocean's bed
Lies, still and lovely, 'mid his voices dread,
Lets his dread currents sweep where'er they list,
Itself in silken tangle hid and kissed.

Time slowly passed ; another evening came,
And still she lay, o'ercome by him they name
Restorer. But, alas! what had he to restore
To one forsaken now for evermore ;
And who knew none of whom she might implore
To live one hour of the loved life of yore ?

Joy could not follow from his realm of dreams,
From lands of unreality, from gleams
Of fancied pleasure to the presence stern
Of fiends whose purpose she might just discern.
Her weakness in its mercy freed a while
The mind from knowledge of their wishes vile,
And let her roam again at will, and smile,
As though this moment opened to her eyes
The home her love had made a paradise.

Her thoughts' fair images still sealed her face,
When a veiled figure entered, and the place
Grew light in evening's dusk, beneath the ray
Of a small lamp that showed the vestments grey
Wherewith the bearer, from her head to feet,
Was closely draped.

             With movements soft and fleet
She came, and paused, and held the lamp on high,
As though in search of one unseen, yet nigh;
Then bent and lowered her arm, when on the floor
She saw an outstretched form, whose stillness bore
A likeness to the lasting rest of death.
But watching closely, she could mark the breath
That made the bosom gently rise and fall,
Could see the love-smile mantling over all,
And stooped to touch her. Starting with a cry,

The captive half arose, as if to fly;
Then, seeing but a woman by her side,
The anxious voice upon her lips had died
Before the visitor had knelt and made
A warning sign, as if of speech afraid.

"Hush!" whispered she, "let no one hear us speak;
Command thy terror,—nay, 'twere best to seek
To keep the smile Sleep brought upon thy cheek:
For thine own sake, for this one night, pretend
That thine alarm to thy content can bend.
Thou look'st upon me as a creature sent
To question, spy, persuade, or to torment:
But see behind this veil; though not as thou,
Time has not drawn the marking on my brow;—
A heavier hand than his, a stronger power,
Has poisoned life, and cursed each wretched hour.
Thus may I claim some fellowship with thee,
For youth and grief belong no less to me.
I come as friend, to counsel and to free,
I come as foe to him thou know'st as foe,—
I come to work him evil, woe for woe.
Hath he not given me enough to make
His grief my pleasure? Never, for thy sake,
Would I perchance deceive him. For mine own
I'll show that Fate obeys not him alone.
Too long, O God, too long, have I obeyed

A force, whose dictates could not be gainsaid,
Though my compliance on my conscience weighed.
And thou too, girl, hadst ne'er the task essayed
To thwart the humours of the tyrant's will.

But though weak flesh may yield, the spirit still
Recoils in hate ; and oft I know again
The bitter pining that is now thy pain ;
For I, like thee, by Moslem pirates ta'en
Was once a Christian ; and the chief shall find
Delight may wither with his altering mind.
He comes to thee this eve,—nay, courage, child,
Thou shalt escape him ! He shall be beguiled
To trust thee. Act the hypocrite a while :
See if thou canst. Thou must not lose thy smile,
But keep it, when thou seest him. I'll be there,
Listen, for 'tis this thou must prepare :
When he shall order me to go, as he
Will surely do, not wishing me with thee,
Then give him this, as if thou didst relent,
When I say "Take it,—from his side I'm sent.'
It is a cup of drink that I prepare,
Refreshing him when past day's toil and care.
And he will take it from thee unaware
That in its freshest foam, a drug lies hid
That, ere a moment passes o'er, will bid
His eyelids fall in slumber, and his arm
Shall be more powerless than thine own for harm."

And as she spoke, came slaves, who for their lord,
Set lights and wine and fruit upon the board ;
And soon El Sirad strode into the room,
Bedecked with gems, and tissues of the loom ;
And greeted both the women, as they stood,
But made the elder a quick sign and rude,
When she, in Lita's hand, with signs of woe,
Placed a full goblet, as she turned to go.

Then Lita, scarcely knowing what she did,
Stretched forth the cup to him, as she was bid ;
That he, in his surprise, took not at first,
Saying, "Beauteous damsel, pray believe my thirst
Was but to see thee reconciled." She came
Yet nearer, choking back her shame
(If shame she felt ;—her manner rather told
Despair had nerved her in her bearing bold) ;
And half instinctively she played the part
On which was set the whole hope of her heart.
She could not raise her eyes ; she could not smile :
He looked at her in silence for a while,
Then drank and said, "I thank thee, and I drink
To happier times, and eyes that shall not sink,
But greet me with their light, when next I come.
Fair sorceress, relent, and be not dumb.
Speak for I'm weary !" And the maid who thought
With horror that the drug no change had wrought,
5

And heard, all agonized with hidden fear,
The loathsome words he spoke as if to cheer,
Now saw him on the cushioned floor reclined,
The thick lips powerless to portray the mind,
The huge form lifeless 'neath the spell of sleep,
The man she so detested, but a heap
Of loosened limbs, his raiment glittering dread
Beneath the light the lamps upon it shed.

Again the woman's voice assailed her ear;
"Great God, he drank it!   Do not idle here.
Leave him, he cannot follow thee.   Now haste,
Arouse thy people, that thy friends may taste
The freedom I may give alone to thee!"

She touched her arm and led her out, and she
Stepped forth in silence down the narrow stair,
Breathed, as amazed, again the outer air,
And halted only, when, without the wall,
She heard the woman's words, "Thou hear'st the fall
Of yonder torrent?   Headlong as its speed
Must be thine own ; and it will safely lead
Down to the woods : then let thy steps be bound
By its lulled murmur,—thus shall Orles be found."

And left alone, she gazed above, where frowned
The black rocks darkly o'er the sombre pines ;

And over them the moon on rugged lines
Of peak and glacier shone, with starlight cold.
And all was quiet, save the stream that told
Of restless haste till home, at last, were found.

Then fled she onward, guided by its sound.
All night she travelled wearily, and yet,
Upon her purpose resolutely set,
With bleeding feet she trod the stones ;—the morn
Still saw the pain with steadfast bravery borne.
But when before her eyes the towers arose
That, in an hour, had yielded her repose ;
And been the dreadful journey's happy close,
Her step swayed, faltering, and her sight grew dim.
Earth, trees, and town appeared to rise, and swim
On misty air, that weighed upon the breast.
Upon her laboring heart a hand was pressed,
As reeling on the bank beside the stream
She fell, and hope seemed but a girlish dream !

'EE, in the heaven there glances,
    Piercing its northern night,
Light, as of luminous lances,
    Flashing, and hurled in fight.

With weird and wavering gleaming
    Bright ranks advance ever higher,
As if through a battle's mist streaming,
    And storming the zenith with fire.

Arrayed like a rainbow, but beating
    The dark, with thousands of spears,
Each thrown, as though armies were meeting,
    All glittering and red re-appears.

At times in fair order, and crossing
    The heaven as with a span,
Or disarrayed, striving, and tossing,
    Seem the hosts to the eyes of man.

See how their lines are shaking,
    Surge on, and fast retire,—

How through them faster breaking
   Rise others,—gleam,—expire.

Are rival banners vying,
   And waved by arméd hands,
Or sheen of planets flying
   From bright celestial brands?

But the silence reigns unbroken,
   They fight without a sound;
If indeed these lights betoken
   That wars the stars astound!

For whether they burn all gory,
   Or blanch the trembling sky,
No thunder vaunts their glory
   As in the gloom they die.

Do they come as warning, telling
   Of death, or war, or shame,
When their tremulous pulses, swelling,
   Can fill the world with flame.

Do they tell of cities burning,
   'Mid sack, and blood, and lust;
Of lighted arrows, turning
   Loved hearths to smoking dust?

For like to an awful presage
　　Of fields of slaughtered dead,
Just where they held their passage
　　A crimson cloud is spread.

Or, boding no fell chastening,
　　Are they but paths, where shine
Swift feet, immortal, hastening
　　With messages divine?

Come thus the angels speeding
　　With blighting wing, and rod?
Ah, none may know the reading
　　Or follow the signs of God!

In silence He, the Maker,
　　Bids kindle the fair fire;
In silence He, the Taker,
　　Lets the red flame expire.

And o'er the watcher's spirit,
　　With Fear, Desire is thrown:
A longing deep doth stir it
　　To know the yet Unknown.

We seek, with useless yearning,
　　To pry at hidden things,

Where God, to mock our learning,
　His veil of mystery flings.

Earth rears us, and to love her
　From birth our nature's bound;
But she, like the fires above her,
　May die without a sound.

Her seasons' varying story,
　The fate of all her race,
May, like the Aurora's glory,
　Change, in a moment's space!

None save the sentry walked the rampart high
Where Guido stood at night with haggard eye,
Thinking in desperate mood upon his love;
When rose that portent in the skies above,
That, seldom seen within a southern clime,
Is held as token of some coming time;
And many a legend tells, "It bodeth woe,
The midnight-dawning of that lambent glow."

The eve had brought him tidings of the raid
That gave to cruel bonds his hapless maid.
Long ere the morning came his fleet would weigh,
And hound the robbers till they turned to bay.

Thus vowed he, raging, and each hour had seen
All fresh equipped, that ne'er had wanting been :
His ships o'erhauled, the bowmen's mantlets swung
Like evil nests, on naked tree-top hung ;
The food was stored, the brawny rowers placed,
The shields made bulwarks for the vessel's waist.
The soldiers crowded on the decks were told
To nurse their vengeance for their vigil cold ;
While their young leader, to take counsel brief,
Left them a while to meet his sire and chief,
Who, overjoyed to see his ardour rise,
Had made him captain of this last emprise.

And soon he joined his son, content to guide
With words, since age would keep him from his side.
Upon the walls that to the seaward faced,
The two, in earnest converse, slowly paced ;
While far above the streamers shot and paled,
The scarlet pinions flapped their plumes, or sailed
Through quivering night, that round them shrunk and
    quailed.

The conference o'er, impatient of delay,
Guido sprang quickly down the rocky way,
Urged his boat's crew, as fast their blades they plied,
Scaled with a shout the largest galley's side,
"Weigh, comrades, weigh! we seek the ocean wide."

Her cables creak, and now the waters, spurned,
And lashed by mighty oars, to foam are churned;
Her ports are shaken by their measured sweep,
And groan responsive to the burdened deep.

But moving soon, as if from slumber woke,
She stirs, she starts at every labouring stroke,
And gathering speed, she darts into the main,
A grim sea-monster, bearing stings of pain,
That myriad-limbed its horrid food will gain.
Her consorts follow in her whitened wake,
Till each, in turn, its destined place can take.

The lights on shore grow dim, the shadows flee
That tell where land leans forth upon the sea.
The slow hours mark the unremitting toil;
And still the stricken waves around must boil
Till morn arise, the winds within her hand
To waft them further from that threatened land.
Meanwhile, despondent on the towering stern,
Guido is learning what it is to earn
Those self-inflicted pangs, when keen Remorse
Gnaws through the heart its agonizing course.
O that a generous fate had earlier shown
The path of Honour, ere the hour was flown
When o'er it Hope could happiness have thrown!
Had he but stemmed the tide of others' woe,

He ne'er had tasted of its sable flow,
Love still remained.—Great God! could it be vain?
Life still was his, her lovely life to gain :
For her, for Vengeance, would he live, and sate
Neglected Justice through a noble hate.
To-morrow's sun should see the billows bleed
Round wrecks that bore the authors of this deed :
Yet how, alas, destruction's bolt to aim
That partial ruin should attend its flame,
And save the captive from revenge and shame?

Another hour the maddening doubt might clear ;
Events might prove it but a causeless fear.
And yet, how terrible the torpid flight
Of Time,—accomplice of forgetful Night!
What meant the rush of those vast wings that spread
A ghostly radiance 'neath the vault o'erhead?
O that they would but blaze upon the seas
Rays that should mark the Paynim as he flees,
And this blind groping with fierce light were smote
To let him fasten on the dastard's throat!
More light! more light! Would morning never come?
Some evil witchery kept the breezes dumb!

No, there they sing, amid the empty shrouds,
The stars are quenched, and rise the rosy clouds!
"Sail, set all sail, we'll gain upon them fast!"

The canvas curtsies to the creaking mast;
A mightier power than human will may wield
Compels her onward o'er the sapphire field.

Her hundred arms are now no longer seen;
Transformed and beauteous, like a sea-born queen,
With gallant grace she glides amid the crowd,
Where the hoarse tumult of rough waves is loud;
And their rude clamour mellows as she speeds,
For a wild wonder to their wrath succeeds.
Lo, their swift ranks are following where she leads,
Their curving crests their offered homage pleads,
Till laughing murmurs their delight reveal
And eddying dances, round the flying keel.

Changed too by love is Guido's stricken soul;
Through his tried spirit have begun to roll
The glorious lights, the mighty gales, that spring
When waking Conscience stirs at last to fling
Pollution from her, though it darkly cling.
Like the fair wind that fills the arching sail,
Love breathes its strength upon his terrors pale;
And makes them serve to bear him straight and true,
Till dangers lessen to his hopeful view;
And former hours seem things of double scorn,
In sight of valour of devotion born.

God speed his course! but ah, will trouble bow
To high resolve, though writ on youthful brow?
Will smiling victory his advances greet,
And following ages his renown repeat?
'Twas not for him to question or decide
Where ebbed the limits of his fortune's tide.
By one thought guided and by one possessed,
The thought that racked him, and in racking blessed,
He scanned the distant line where wave on wave
Sharp cruel teeth to bare horizon gave,
And turned in bitterness away, as nought
His straining vision to his senses brought,
And through the watches of the morn, the light
But mocked the yearning of the feverish night.

The wind increases; the flotilla strown
Far o'er the seas is tossed apart, and thrown
From swelling ridges whence the world is seen,
To lonely hollows walled with waters green.
Swift ragged clouds eclipse the sea and sky,
And by the staggering ship pass shrieking by,
That reels forsaken, save by one sea mew:
A creature hailed as comrade by the crew,
And watched by Guido till his fancy gives
Mysterious meaning to the thing that lives
Borne on the breast of tempests, as a child
Is dandled in caress of mother mild;

And looking on it, as with scarce a beat
Of its long wings it follows him through heat
Of noon and cold of night, on pinious fleet :
With utterance low his restless thought finds speech,
And broken tones no listening ear may reach :—

I.

While through the roaring surf I sail
    To track the coward rover,
One ensign to my mast I nail
    To float till life be over.

II.

And thou, sharp-winged and milk-white bird,
    Who followest ever after,
Whose wild notes o'er the deep are heard
    Above the hoarse waves' laughter;

III.

Art thou indeed, as seems to me,
    Her spirit, sorrow-laden,
Sent forth, in longing, o'er the sea,—
    The spirit of my maiden?

An answering blast with omen sad replies,
The bird departs with loud and wailing cries ;
The day wanes quickly, and another time

Of hateful doubt must hide the men of crime ;
But danger comes as giver of relief,
And makes the busy hours by contrast brief.

Amid the foam that they at dawn descry,
They see a vessel that no more can fly :.
From shattered stumps mere strips of canvas stream,
The high waves beat through many an opened seam,
And fling their froth, as serpents lick their prey,
O'er the doomed hull ere hiding it from day ;

Her low-laid length the corsair craft betrays :
O God of justice, to Thy name be praise!
With weapons bared, and with exultant cheers,
The Christian bark upon the foeman steers ;
Grapples her quarter, pours upon her beam
A clattering torrent, a fierce leaping stream
Of armed avengers, for an instant checked,
Then pouring headlong o'er resistance wrecked.

Faint words, from lips of dying wretches wrung,
Tell how all hope on false delusion hung.
How the swift sails they thought they had pursued,
Might now from Orles indeed be closely viewed,
But that none lingered on the storm-swept sea.
One ship alone of all, by Heaven's decree,
This sinking hull, by lightning struck and maimed,

By friends forsaken when their aid she claimed,
Would fail in that thick fringe of mast and spar
That round the harbour forms a fatal bar
'Gainst Christian fleets, to keep their succour far ;
One band alone of all the Prophet's host,
That but embarked to swoop upon the coast,
Would ne'er take part in that victorious march
That sets the keystone to proud Islam's arch ;
That arch of conquest, 'neath whose shelter cast,
Orles' captive daughters shall forget the past.

Enough, enough, the impious boast had breath
From hearts now shielded from revenge by death ;
Quick sword-thrusts cannot jest, nor yet that fire
That gave the infidel a hissing pyre,
Where flame and wave, commingling, fought to win,
Like fiends that battle for lost souls of sin.

But did not Truth the ghastly fiction spurn,
Must fell Despair embitter the return ;
Leave other hearts to joy in harvests sown
By those whose grief no carnage could atone?

The cowering dread that bids the partridge lie
'Mid dust or leaf while yet the hawk is nigh ;
The fatal panic that so closely holds
The victim menaced by the serpent's folds ;

The vague yet strong foreboding of his doom
At times vouchsafed the traveller to the tomb;
Appeared to brood upon the steep-built town
Since reddening skies had told of heaven's frown,
And her stout manhood, lured by guile to fly,
Had left the helpless to withstand and die.

The few who on their errands, hasting, went,
Seemed worn by sorrow, and with toiling spent;
No prattling children chased with eager feet
As wont of yore, the passer in the street;
Her women, wan and trembling in distress,
Could find no hand to comfort them and bless;
For e'en old soldiers, left behind, would prose
No more of early fightings, joys, or woes;
But in grave silence donned the weighty steel,
And marvelled time had made it heavier feel
Than when, with youth and confidence elate,
They saw themselves the guardians of the State,
Where now sad auguries alone held reign
That e'en the boldest had not dared disdain.

Her caverned ways lay hushed where'er they wound,
And from the church alone was heard the sound
Of voices raised, that in united prayer
Breathed low responses to the listening air;
While the robed priests from rise to set of sun

Prayed God his suppliants not in wrath to shun,
But in His strength invincible to rise
And show His mercy to His servants' eyes.

What varying signs, what altering moods attest
The presence stern of that unwelcome guest
Who seeks at times an entry to each breast;
Who, lodged within the fortress he has ta'en,
Tears down disguises men assume in vain;
Whose hand, of ice, can thrill through nerve and bone,
Can prove our nature by one touch alone;
Can still the wildest, and the fiercest tame,
By might that Fear and Fear alone can claim!

No sentient life, inheriting the dower
Of thought or instinct, can deny its power.
A gift of God to warn the weak of harm,
And move the valour of the stronger arm;
And yet an influence giving rise to care
Too great for frail humanity to bear,
Deepening our evil till its gloom is far
Too dense and dark for virtue's high-set star;
But 'mid the night how bright the silvery glow
On all, soul-lifted, o'er the world below!
No craven he, who has to fear confessed,
Nor brave the man whom it has ne'er oppressed;
For he who knows it not, is less than brute,

6

He wretch alone, who lets its terrors root,
He bravest only, who, with courage high,
Feels the full risk, and mans himself to die!

Lita was safe, if safety could be said
To live in hearing of fell danger's tread,
And she, for once a prophetess of ill,
Had brought the warning they neglected still;
For paralyzed by all her lips disclosed,
A deadening fear each energy opposed.

Some peasants journeying in the early morn
To pluck their citrons, found the maid forlorn,
Still senseless by the stream; then quickly borne
Upon their mule into the town, her life
Came back, to warn them of the coming strife.
They brought her in, and sent unto their lord,
Who came to test the news that spread abroad.

Then she, in this extremity but made
Calm by the peril she had well essayed,
In clear and rapid narrative, could tell
The threats she heard, and what to her befell.
And thus it chanced that for his town's defence,
The aged warrior counsel took, from whence
Others had found in moments of distress
The strength of innocence, and gentleness.

And seeing she was resolute to bear
In man's misfortune woman's heavy share,
He told how straitly they were then beset;
Nor found her cheek with idle tear grow wet,
But kindle with quick blood as she inquired
If feeble arms, by his example fired,
Might not assist the fighters on the wall,
Where levers plied, give rock-like stones their fall;
Or if young eyes could not best watch and mark
The points most threatened in the masking dark?

And he, enamoured of her spirit, showed
How, though her strength could never swell the load
Of heavy stones that, piled on wall and tower,
Would plunge, to shatter the assailant's power,
Yet the black caldrons filled with boiling oil,
And smoking pitch must prove her helpful toil;
If rain of darts but came from clouds of men,
Few arms could shower these simpler weapons; then
Her aid, with those she could persuade and guide,
Might kindle numerous watch-fires, so their pride
Would seem unto the foe as though displayed
By many bands, in order firm arrayed.
Young eyes could watch the movements of the night;
Quick hands bring water, if a sudden light
Among the houses spoke of bursting flame.

And by the evening, she had roused the shame
Of weeping wives and maids, while wall and keep
Were weighted well with many a rough stone heap.
The molten missiles glowed in vessels deep,
And some security with pain was gained.
Thus aided she the burghers who remained,
Who half distraught, had with the veterans made
Within each gate a sturdy barricade,
And when the water tanks were filled, their work was done
But as they lit the fires at set of sun,
They saw rise dimly on the moaning sea
The pirate fleet, that found the harbour free
Of all defence. The crews soon inland stole
And left their ships at the abandoned mole.

Then flared the watch-fires on the rampart height,
And gave the town a coronet of light;
And the grim host whose troops had poured around,
Ranked in deep columns on the teeming ground,
Illumined by the blaze, recoiled as though
Surprised and startled at a ready foe:
And the beleaguered, staring into night,
Stood back appalled at their besiegers' might;
For the bright glare, from every spear returned,
On the mailed ranks, again repeated, burned.

But 'mid the Saracens the cry arose,
Prudence forbade them in such haste to close,

When thus the garrison was seen prepared.
No false attacks their weaknesses had bared,
And there was reason stratagem to fear:
Was the port opened but to lure them near?
Sirad had died: was all then evil-starred
That came from him; had e'en his plans been marred,
Their purport reached the town? Perhaps there lay
The vessels they had thought decoyed away,
In ambush, hid within some neighbouring bay?

Thus by their fear, 'twixt doubt and longing tost,
With their best leader to their guidance lost,
They paused, suspicious, and their anchors weighed;
And standing off the port a while, displayed
Their seaward strength. Thus, circling all the place,
They waited, turning unto Orles their face.

A welcome breathing time! although unknown, .
Its worth supreme to those, to whom alone
It seemed a marvel, and a respite brief;
For they could count upon no late relief,
But waited, wondering if from sea or land
Should come the stroke God dealt with heavy hand?

But at the hour when Guido, far away,
Knowing their need, fled back for rescue; they
Saw the ringed armament around them move,

As though at last their poor defence to prove;
And crawling slowly o'er the land, on sea
It glided almost imperceptibly,
Till the space narrowed to a bowshot's length,
That intervened 'twixt gallantry and strength.

Then suddenly upon three points was made
The Paynims' onslaught, while their trumpets brayed;
And their short arrows showered upon the wall,
Thick as from pines the brown dead needles fall.
Just where 'tis lowest, and they deem it weak,
They throw their grapnels and an entry seek
With light rope ladders that, beneath their weight,
Sway with the struggling of the living freight;
At the two gates assailing masses throng,
With beams and hammers, thundering loud and long,
Till in its rivets shakes each structure strong.
But by the battlements protected well,
The answering bowmen can the slaughter swell:
Their hissing shafts whirr swiftly, seeking blood,
And, striking deeply, taste the crimson flood;
While thundering loudly down on shield and helm,
The rugged stones the foremost foemen whelm,
And the loud roar of the assaulting host
Is met by cheers that ring along the coast.

The climbing swarms, from broken ladders thrown,
In writhing remnants clutch the ground and groan.

But lo! the earth for every parting life
Yields three, to lavish on the desperate strife:
Again the storming parties, mounting, vie
To seize the wall, and when the top is nigh,
Are downward hurled, with hatred's yelling cry,
And bite the dust, 'mid dying men to die!
The reeling press gives way a while, aghast
At the grim havoc death can deal so fast;
Then rallying to the war-cry, feared of old,
Onward once more the tide of battle rolled;
Above their heads their serried shields they hold,
Amid the dust that rises like a cloud,
Again attacking; on their maddened crowd
The ponderous missiles drop in deadly hail,
In vain: no, see, they halt; they break, they quail!
The noon has come to watch the work accurst,   .
And vex the wounded with a tenfold thirst;
When overworn with weariness and heat,
The hostile columns make a slow retreat.
The earth-born vapours that in air were tost
By gleams from moving armour pierced, and crossed,
Now rise no more from off the trampled ground.
The battle's voices cease; and far around
Nature, beneficent and peaceful, brings
The holy calm, that broods beneath her wings.
On soundless shore, and sleeping sea, she reigns,
O'er the hushed mountains and the silent plains;

For one short hour, throughout the beauteous scene
Violence has yielded to her sway serene.

But men whose words were bravest, and whose cry
Was ever, "Courage, fight! ye see they fly!"
Know that the strain is more than can be borne,
If such a night again bring such a morn;
And yet undaunted, the old knight has turned
Again to Lita, saying, "Thou hast earned
More than thy share of glory, but the means
Thou hast prepared for victory, though she leans
As if bestowing upon us the palm,
Are not enough.   The foe has wrought no harm
Upon our buildings, for his wild desire
For plunder shielded them from shafts of fire.
These, at the next attack, will surely fly
Upon the roofs. See there! as if to try
My words, they come with torches, and the bows
Already in the front, the danger grows!
Then be it thine, with all thy comrades here,
To stifle with quick hands this flickering fear,
That soon shall threaten us in front and rear.
Be this thy work; and if I send to tell
That we are pressed too sorely, see thou well
That all the women, though they wail their loss,
Leave gear and goods as if they were but dross,
And instant seek the castle; there we may

Yet reckon with them for our toil to-day :
Now to the wells, for we must to the wall."

Then while her band, obedient to her call,
Wait near the tanks, and in the shelter cower,
Hoping 'gainst hope to mar the flames dread power,
A herald, springing to the Moorish van,
Cries for surrender! "or the winds shall fan
Destruction o'er each dwelling, and each man
Shall die by sword, or fire." To whom the knight,
Standing conspicuous on the blood-stained height,
Replies disdainfully, "No sun shall see,
No stars behold such dastard infamy ;"
Daring the worst. And as the torches dance
Among the Arab ranks, their files advance :
And singly placed afar, they slowly bend
The bows, and overhead, high-aimed, they send
The first red arrow, with its trail of flame.

And following flights incessant seek the same
High paths, and arching in wide curves the air,
Fall crackling on the tiles, or lighting where
The woodwork, wrinkled by the sun, is bare,
Strike with dulled stroke : and anxiously aware
Of the great peril menacing so near,
The few defenders of the wall, for fear
Of fresh attack, durst never quit their post,

But idly watching the opposing host,
And all inactive, marked with added gloom
The fiery messengers of coming doom.

But where the tongues of leaping heat would rise,
Warned by prompt signal, bred of watchful eyes,
The ready water, hissing o'er the roof,
Still kept the dwelling to the peril proof.
But as the evening came, the sneaking fire
Rose at one spot yet higher still and higher;
And in attempting to subdue its might,
Amid the arrows' ever quickening flight,
Some of the women by the shafts were maimed.
And then came panic, as the houses flamed,
And a wild onset from the foe without,
And hurried tumult, with blind rage and doubt.

The strong resistance was no more; o'erdone,
Outnumbered, and exhausted, as the sun
Descended sadly, the survivors let
The growing conflict follow, as they set
Their faces to the castle, and arrayed
In such fair order that no haste betrayed
Dismay was spreading 'mid their ranks, they closed
Gates that deaf iron to grim threats opposed.

There for an instant, by their victory fired,
To win the bridge the furious foe aspired.

But where two warriors scarce could keep abreast
Numbers were useless; and no foot could rest
Upon its narrow path, where every rock
Thrown from the fortress overhead, with shock
That seemed enough to crush its slender build,
Would fall; and rolling over where the way was filled
With daring men, would leave it bare and clean,
Save for the blood that on its dust was seen:
As though mere flies had thus been brushed away,
Where shrinking souls had left the mangled clay,
That hurled to the abyss beneath, lay stilled,
Forgotten in the place its life had filled.
For soon, withdrawing from the fatal space,
Where lay the bravest of their dauntless race,
The Moorish host among the houses spread,
And in the Christian homes, untenanted,
Sought eagerly for spoil, and of the wine
Made glad carousal.

    Then the gleaming line
That marked the limits of the fire's domain
Spread out and lengthened slowly, until fain
To force their rival conqueror to delay,
They stayed his course; but threw with waste away
The water gathered in the town, that none
Remained at last when victory was won.
From smouldering embers, from the parching glow,

They turned athirst to greet the wine's cool flow;
And drank, till revelry and riot rung
Through the thick darkness that o'er Orles was hung;
For smoke from burning roofs and buildings' fall
Spread through the night a dim, gigantic pall.
And 'neath its shadow, Sleep swept down to stand
Upon the ramparts, and to wave his hand;
And impious mouths were closed, and fevered brows,
That flushed at braggart and blaspheming vows,
Relaxed in still forgetfulness, as though
The spell that held them could no breaking know.

But 'neath the robe of silence that she wore,
Night in her womb a ghastly danger bore;
For the hot ashes, kindling at the breath
Of whispering breezes, subtly wrought for death.
And where they slumbered in the timber's heart,
Through blackened surfaces began to start;
Until with lurid hue incarnadined,
A pulsing life replaced the darkness blind;
And greeting with hot lips the outer air,
Caressed it, rising from its steaming lair,
With fair and lustrous arms, that felt and sought
The ambient element that vigour brought,
And fed on its desire; then flung on high
Broad beckoning banners to the answering sky;
And onward leaping, urged afar and near
The rapid ravage of a fell career.

In stupor sunk, by dull oblivion doomed,
The Paynim soldier sleeps, until entombed,
And many an agony and stifled groan
Is seen and heard by vengeful flames alone.
The blaze, extending with devouring rage,
Aroused the rest a useless fight to wage.
Where yet a hope remains they soon create
A line of ruin, barren, desolate,
And seek to mock their grim pursuer's greed
By leaving nought whereon his tongue may feed.
But as they toil to gain a narrow space,
And pray destruction may avert its face ;
The paltry trenches are o'erleaped and stormed,
The conflagration o'er each house has formed
A dazzling pile of forked and stabbing fires,
Like hellish phantoms, shaped as shrines and spires.

But round the church's tower and shining roof
Still guardian angels kept the fiends aloof ;
And from the keep, the Christians could behold
How, as the bellowing flames about it rolled,
The ancient fane, around its massive wall,
Gave hope and refuge, still alike, to all.
As there the Saracens stood thronged in light,
Or fled yet further into blackest night,
Out of the darkness, and from off the sea
Were wafted sounds, that made men bend the knee

To pray they told of conflict, and to hear
If aid they meant, and if they drew more near;
And spring again to foot, and grasp their arms,
For such sharp notes must speak of war's alarms.

Aid comes! aid comes, oh, hark the surging cry
The quick assault sends forth unto the sky!
Hark! as if oaks were crashing in the blast
The splintering ruin of some tangling mast,
The shock of charging prows; the ringing knell
Of whose hushed notes the mournful wave must tell!

Oh, who can know the fortunes of the fight,
Interpreting the doubt of doom aright?
And who distinguish 'mid that awful din
The battle-call, that shall, prevailing, win?
Yet, as the tumult to their ears is borne,
Joy may re-enter every heart forlorn;
Returning strength sustain the shaking knees,
"Orles, Orles!" and "Rescue!" vibrate on the breeze;
"Orles, Orles!" replies the knight, and shouts amain,
"Down with the dogs! who follows me again?"

The fighting passion of his early days
Burns in his veins, and sheds on age its rays.
The gates are opened and a faithful few
Charge, and with him the conflict they renew.

Against the flying foe his band he leads,
But when the church is reached, he falls, he bleeds!

Meanwhile the Fates, inexorable, brought
Recoiling mischief back to where 'twas wrought.
Expelled by terrors they themselves contrived,
Of Orles' strong shelter suddenly deprived, ·
The Moslems, scattered in disorder, meet
A death too merciful, because too fleet.

But, springing o'er their prostrate corpses, who
Comes swift, as though on wingéd foot he flew?
Whose the tall form with pallid face that speeds
Before the foremost where the vanguard leads?
Who passes now the bridge, and now the gate,
And pauses only where the women wait,
A piteous crowd on floor of court and stair,
And seems to seek, but seek for one not there?
Though numbers press in every vaulted space,
All seems a void without that absent face,
Each passage empty, and he rushes down
Again to wander in the burning town.

Look, his wild eye with quick delight can beam;
For by the church, and near the fountain's stream,
Is she for whom he seeks, nor seeks in vain,
For Lita turns not from his arms again!

But soon her hand points where his father lies ;
And Guido starts, and flies to him, and tries
To chase the blood to nerveless fingers, laid
Upon the handle of a crimsoned blade ;
Then notes how carefully a scarf is bound
And fastened firmly where the wound is found ;
Sees how the eyelids lift their heavy fringe
And faintly life again the cheeks may tinge.
The ashen lips with feeble effort smile,
As Lita kneels by Guido's side the while,
And looking on his son, and on the maid,
"Let nought against thy love for her be said."
He slowly speaks, "She came to bind my hurt,
She brought the warning to our town inert,
She reft the infidel of Sirad's aid,
Her timely help the battle's chances swayed ;
By her the fire throughout the day was stayed,
And safe retreat ensured to wife and maid.
What say these people, are they ours? My sight
Grows dim.   O place me 'neath the altar bright."

And borne by soldiers come from victory's fight
They lay him where afresh the candles burn
Beneath the crucifix, that he may turn
His dying gaze upon the Death Divine.

And as the shades of night at length incline
To tints of grey, the rescued people meet,

And kneel in church, or search if fervid heat
Has spared some relic they may fondly greet.
But, with the flushing of the rising sun
On sea, and mount, and clouds of smoke-wreaths dun,
Is heard a cry from those who, where they stand,
See the white line of bay-indented strand.

They point to where, along the western road
Bright pennons wave, and brilliant horsemen goad
Their steeds, with ardour, o'er the winding way.
Light leaps and ripples o'er their long array,
A silver river, kissed by joyous day!
Whence come those troops, whose glittering ranks appear
An endless host, although the van is near?
Moors would not ride so frankly, and so free
On Christian land, by Orles' well guarded sea?
'Tis not a foeman who thus comes? Behold,
He bears a banner with a cross of gold!

Each heart may joy, and sheathed be every sword:
There rides our Liege, Provence's sovereign Lord! (²)
Away with grief, let every fear be banned,
Our Prince is come, the Father of our land,
Count William comes, with chivalry, with might,
Isarn, blessed Prelate! rides upon his right.
Forth then to meet him, through our blackened gates,
And greet the vengeance that the Moor awaits!

The gallant train the church's front has gained;
Their Leader's steed is at the fountain reined,
And Guido takes his Lord within to view;
Him whom he mourns, the sire the Paynim slew,
Recounts the tale of those adventurous days,
How brief their space, and yet it years outweighs!
When all is learned, the Count goes forth to stand
Upon the church's steps, and lifts his hand,
And bids his troops rank round him on the place;
And calls for Lita, who, with blushing face
Comes out to stand before him; and he speaks:
"Who now for glory, or for honour seeks,
Let him, from deeds done here, example take;
Deeds of this gentle maiden, whom I make
A Lady of my land, and ask that she
Attend my court: and Guido, as for thee,
Thou too must follow; till the realm be free
Of heathen hordes, our swords must never sleep.
Our name must be so terrible, yon deep
Shall yet refuse to bear upon its breast
The fleets it brought to startle us from rest."

Thus by his love was Guido called to brave
War on the land, and war upon the wave.
By love awakened to a manly pride,
In spirit searched, and changed, and purified,
His bright renown o'er Christendom was spread,
And lived where'er the light of victory sped.

A year has passed, and where red battle burned,
Fair Peace again with blessings has returned,
And mailed processions, banished from the field,
To white-robed trains the festive town must yield.
See, to the sound of music and of song,
A stately pageant slowly moves along.
Before the church's door the crowds divide;
Hail the sweet pomp, that guards the maiden bride!
Hail the young lord, who comes this day to claim,
A prize, the guerdon of a glorious name!
They kneel before the altar, hand in hand,
While thronged around, Provence's warriors stand.

Hush! for the sacred rites, the solemn vow,
That crowns with Faith, young Love's impetuous brow.
The prayer is said; then, as the anthem swells
A peal rings out of happy marriage bells;
Grief pales and dies 'neath joy's ascending sun,
For knight, and maid, have blent their lives in one.

NOTES.

(¹) "Le midi ne fut plus assailli par de grandes armées d'infidèles ; (after 924 A. D.) mais, durant près d'un demi-siècle encore, la côte de Provence et les défilés des Alpes furent infestés par la colonie de brigands musulmans qui s'étaient fait un repaire inaccessible dans les bois et les rochers de Freycinet ou la Garde-Frainet, non loin de Saint-Tropez, et du golfe de Grimaud. Ces audacieux bandits s'emparèrent de tous les passages qui mènent de la Gaule en Italie, pénétrèrent de vallée en vallée jusque dans le Valais, l'Helvétie et la Lombardie, et s'établirent au couvent de Saint-Maurice en 940. Les pèlerins de Rome, longtemps dépouillés ou massacrés par eux, finirent par leur payer un tribut régulier, analogue à celui que les hadjis de la Mecque ont si longtemps payé aux Arabes du désert. Ils occupaient une multitude de tours et de forteresses, depuis les sources du Rhône jusqu'à l'embouchure du Var ; ils étaient devenus une puissance politique, et se ménageaient entre le roi d'Italie et le roi d'Arles, qui craignaient également de les pousser à bout."—*Histoire de France,* par MARTIN. Tom. ii. p. 510.

(²) "On ignore s'il se passa quelques événements dignes d'intérêt dans la France romane de 966 à 973 ; on sait seulement que les chefs provençaux, durant cette intervalle, chassèrent et détruisirent glorieusement les bandes musulmanes qui avaient si longtemps rançonné leur pays, et que la politique des rois d'Italie avait protégées pour rendre l'accès des Alpes plus difficile aux hommes de France et de Germanie. Les Sarrasins n'avaient pu tenir longtemps le poste de Saint-Maurice, ce point central des Alpes qu'ils avaient envahi avec une si étonnante audace ; mais ils conservaient toujours de nombreux repaires dans les Basses-Alpes, et surtout dans les rochers de Fraxinet, capitale de cette république de pirates : Guilhem, comte d'Arles ou de Provence, secondé, suivant les traditions locales, par un prélat guerrier, Isarn, évêque de Grenoble, détruisit successivement ces aires d'oiseaux de proie, et finit par écraser les 'infidèles' dans un combat décisif, au moment où ils se repliaient de toutes parts sur Fraxinet : la colonie musulmane fut tout entière taillée en pièces ou engloutie dans les précipices de ces côtes abruptes."—*Histoire de France*, par MARTIN. Tom. ii. p. 535.